PUFFIN B

THE REAL THING

Tom Palmer is a football fan and a writer. He never did well at school. But once he got into reading about football – in newspapers, magazines and books – he decided he wanted to be a football writer more than anything. As well as the Football Academy series, he is the author of the Football Detective series, also for Puffin Books.

Tom lives in a Yorkshire town called Todmorden with his wife and daughter. The best stadium he's visited is Real Madrid's Santiago Bernabéu.

Find out more about Tom on his website *tompalmer.co.uk*

Books by Tom Palmer

Football Academy series:

BOYS UNITED

STRIKING OUT

THE REAL THING

READING THE GAME

For older readers

FOOTBALL DETECTIVE: FOUL PLAY

FOOTBALL DETECTIVE: DEAD BALL

TOM PALMER

FOOTBALL ACADEMY

THE REAL THING

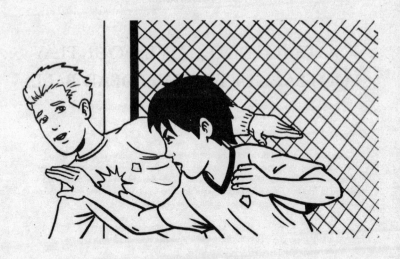

Illustrated by
Brian Williamson

PUFFIN

PUFFIN BOOKS

Published by the Penguin Group

Penguin Books Ltd, 80 Strand, London WC2R ORL, England

Penguin Group (USA) Inc., 375 Hudson Street, New York, New York 10014, USA

Penguin Group (Canada), 90 Eglinton Avenue East, Suite 700, Toronto, Ontario, Canada M4P 2Y3
(a division of Pearson Penguin Canada Inc.)

Penguin Ireland, 25 St Stephen's Green, Dublin 2, Ireland (a division of Penguin Books Ltd)

Penguin Group (Australia), 250 Camberwell Road, Camberwell, Victoria 3124, Australia
(a division of Pearson Australia Group Pty Ltd)

Penguin Books India Pvt Ltd, 11 Community Centre, Panchsheel Park, New Delhi – 110 017, India

Penguin Group (NZ), 67 Apollo Drive, Rosedale, North Shore 0632, New Zealand
(a division of Pearson New Zealand Ltd)

Penguin Books (South Africa) (Pty) Ltd, 24 Sturdee Avenue, Rosebank,
Johannesburg 2196, South Africa

Penguin Books Ltd, Registered Offices: 80 Strand, London WC2R ORL, England

puffinbooks.com

First published 2009

015

Text copyright © Tom Palmer, 2009
Illustrations copyright © Brian Williamson, 2009
All rights reserved

The moral right of the author and illustrator has been asserted

Set in Baskerville MT 14.5/21 pt by Palimpsest Book Production Limited,
Grangemouth, Stirlingshire
Made and printed in England by Clays Ltd, Elcograf S.p.A

British Library Cataloguing in Publication Data
A CIP catalogue record for this book is available from the British Library

ISBN: 978-0-141-32469-2

www.greenpenguin.co.uk

MIX
Paper from
responsible sources
FSC
www.fsc.org   FSC™ C018179

Penguin Books is committed to a sustainable
future for our business, our readers and our planet.
This book is made from Forest Stewardship
Council™ certified paper.

For Jim Sells and Ralph Newbrook,
the ultimate strike partnership

Contents

The Real Thing

'What is that?'

Ryan was standing in the doorway of the dressing room, his bag over his shoulder. His friend Ben was standing next to him. Although Ryan was talking to Tomasz, United's goalkeeper, he really wanted the whole room to hear.

'A football shirt,' Tomasz said in a quiet but firm voice.

Eight other boys watched and listened; they were sitting on the benches around the

1

edge of the dressing room. Most of them were still in their normal clothes.

'No, *this* is a football shirt,' Ryan said, pulling his jumper off, displaying the latest Real Madrid top. It was white with purple trim.

Tomasz's top was white with black trim. The club badge read 'Legia Warsaw'. It was the team he had always supported. And it was the team he missed since he had moved to England with his parents over a year ago.

'Nice top,' Ben said, looking Ryan up and down.

'And who are Legia Warsaw?' Ryan said, ignoring his friend.

'My team,' Tomasz said calmly.

'Never heard of them,' Ryan said. 'Are they Polish by any chance?'

A couple of the boys sitting down laughed.

James – one of the team's central defenders – had been listening to the conversation from the corner of the dressing room. He stood up and walked towards Ryan and Ben. He was the team's steadiest influence. He was also the son of a former England international.

'Leave it,' James said.

Ben stepped back. He always did what

James said, even more than he did what Ryan said.

Ryan was about to say something to James but Steve, the team manager, came in. Whatever it was he had to say would have to wait.

'Right, lads,' Steve announced.

Steve had been the manager of United's under-twelves for three years. The team he coached were all on schoolboy contracts at United's famous Academy, a huge complex of buildings and football pitches on the outskirts of the town. The team included some of the best young players of their age group. Some were from that town, others from further away. The cream of them – those who worked hard – would become professional footballers one day.

Tomasz sat back, relieved. He'd been saved from another load of hassle from

Ryan. Ryan: team captain. Ryan: team bully. Tomasz could think about the game now.

Today United were playing Newcastle at home – a friendly against another Premiership under-twelve side.

Steve went on: 'This lot are a good team. They've won every game they've played this season. They pass the ball around really nicely.' Steve looked at Ryan. 'A bit like your precious Real Madrid.'

Ryan grinned.

Steve was famous for his deep voice. If you heard it coming across a football pitch, you listened to it. And if he was doing a team talk you took in every word – and did lots of nodding.

'So what we need today is teamwork,' Steve continued. 'If anyone's playing at fifty per cent today we'll be exposed. But as long

as we play *together*, as a team, and look after each other, we'll be all right.'

The boys nodded and started to get changed.

This season they'd played seven games, winning four, drawing one and losing two. A good start.

But Newcastle at home was going to be the hardest game yet.

Tough

After ten minutes of the game, it was still nil–nil. United had done well. Newcastle could pass the ball, but they'd not got behind Ryan and his defence.

'They're not so good,' Ryan said to Ben after the ball had gone out for a throw-in.

Ben laughed. 'Easy,' he said.

James went to take the throw-in, standing close to the halfway line.

Ryan ran casually to trap the ball, but a Newcastle player came out of nowhere, beating him to it. Ryan tried to take his legs, but he was too quick.

Once he had the ball, the Newcastle player – a huge blond boy – took two strides and passed the ball to a team-mate. Then he was running. His team-mate looked up, saw his run, and fed the ball back to him. Suddenly the blond player was in the penalty area, already past United's two central defenders, Ryan and James.

Tomasz had no chance.

The striker clipped the ball over him as he ran out to close down the angles.

As the Newcastle players wheeled away to celebrate, Ryan could hear Steve shouting his name. He tried not to listen, but couldn't avoid his deep booming voice.

'Ryan . . . concentrate . . . teamwork.'

He could also hear his mum shouting. Again.

Ryan's mum was difficult – *forever* shouting at him, the referee and other players, telling them what to do. He could just imagine what she'd be saying. He shut the voices out and jogged over to Tomasz.

'You're not playing for Legia Whatever-they're-called now, Tomasz,' Ryan said. 'You should have closed the striker down. There was time to.' He was angry. His thoughts short and sharp.

Tomasz said nothing. He knew Ryan was at fault for the goal. He should have been marking the blond striker more closely.

The next time Newcastle attacked, Tomasz felt his confidence draining away. This team they were playing were passing the ball so quickly. And they were all so huge and

strong. United didn't have a chance. *He* didn't have a chance.

Again the United defence were cut in two. Again Tomasz was left one-on-one with the blond striker. And again, seconds later, he was picking the ball out of the back of the net.

By half-time it was three–nil to Newcastle.

Steve was not impressed.

'There's something wrong here,' he said. 'Newcastle are good, yes, but not *that* much better than us. We need teamwork.' He sighed. 'Look at how they are passing and moving. Anticipating each other's space and runs. *We* can do that. We've been doing it all season.'

Steve looked at his team, sitting in a circle round him. He'd never seen them look like this. *Confused* was the first word that came into his head.

'First, it's possession,' he said. 'The more time we have the ball, the less they have it. Defenders? Pass it out – don't hoof it.'

Steve looked at Tomasz.

The keeper was afraid of what he was going to say. He'd never conceded three goals in a half before in his life. In Poland *or* in England. He felt like he didn't have any confidence, that every attack was going to end with him beaten.

'Tomasz needs *protecting*,' Steve said. 'The three goals . . . he had no chance. He was exposed.' Steve paused, then went on. 'I need defenders defending. Deep, if necessary. Midfielders overlapping back if a defender is committed to an attack. Agreed?'

There were nods of agreement. A couple of the lads said, 'Yes, Steve.'

Ryan sat and listened. He hadn't dared look at his mum since the second goal went in. She was lurking fifty metres away, but under strict orders from Steve not to come any closer during the match or the half-time team talk. He dreaded what she would say to him in the car on the way home.

'Right then,' Steve said, catching Ryan's eye. 'Let's get out there. We can win the half. That's your target now.'

As the rest of the boys ran back on to the pitch, Steve called Ryan over. 'I need you to set an example, Ryan,' he said. 'Concentrate. And teamwork. Yeah?'

Ryan nodded. And running on to the pitch, he wondered whether Steve had meant to criticize him – or ask him to lead the team more like a captain was meant to.

Ready to Go

'**D**oes anyone have anything else to add?' Steve said, after going through the Newcastle game with the players.

It had been hard. Not like any after-match chat they'd had before.

And that was because they'd lost five–one.

Tomasz had kept quiet throughout the chat. He was feeling something like shame. But a bit of anger too. He'd been the

keeper who had let all five goals in. But it was how Ryan had made him feel that really hurt. The way he went on and on at him.

'But let's say no more about the game,' Steve said. 'Overall, the second half was much better. Far closer. We almost matched them. And they've thrashed most teams they've played this year.'

Tomasz looked around the room. Most of his team-mates had their heads down, looking at the floor or their kitbags. It was the worst result of the season. A season that was supposed to be getting better, Tomasz thought.

'Come on, lads,' Steve said, a laugh in his voice. 'We've talked it through and gone over what we can learn from the game today. And . . . we've got a European tournament to worry about now.'

All the players suddenly looked up. Frowns had turned into smiles. The boys were looking at each other, grinning. It felt like Steve had flicked a switch in the room. The happy switch.

'That's better,' Steve said. 'And I'm pleased to say the whole team is coming. All of you.'

Steve looked at Yunis and smiled.

Yunis, the team's leading scorer, smiled back. He'd thought he wasn't going to make it until the last minute. But his dad had come through in the end – and said he *could* go, after all.

'Now then,' Steve said. 'Who's been to Poland before?'

Tomasz's hand shot up.

'Tell us about it, Tomasz. When did you leave Poland to come here?'

'Just a year ago.'

'And you played for Legia Warsaw?'

'No, I played for Lodz. But I support Legia.'

'I see,' Steve said. 'And what is it like in Poland?'

'It's good. Very friendly people.'

'That's important, Tomasz. It leads me on to what I want to say. Thank you.'

Steve looked serious for a moment. Then he continued: 'That's because I want this tournament to be a good one on two

17

levels. One, for football, of course. We're playing some big teams. AC Milan under-twelves. Real Madrid under-twelves. And Legia Warsaw.'

Ryan sniggered quietly.

Tomasz looked at him, puzzled. What was he laughing at now?

Steve glanced at Ryan. 'Something to say, Ryan?'

Ryan smirked. 'No. Nothing.'

'Good. Because the second important thing I want to say is what Tomasz highlighted. *Friendliness*.' Steve shifted his feet and folded his arms. 'All of you – *and* that includes me and the other adults who are coming – are going out there for some fun, to play football. But we must never forget that, first and foremost, we are representing United. Everything we do and say reflects on the good name of the club. We're a big

name in Europe – a well-respected name.
And I want it to stay that way. Any trouble
and I will get to the bottom of it. And I will
take action.'

All the players looked at Steve, but no
one spoke.

Steve smiled. 'Look, you're a good
bunch. I don't expect any trouble. And the
last thing I want to do is put a dampener
on the trip. I know you're all excited. But I
have to say this.'

Connor, one of the defenders, signed from an Irish league team a year earlier, put his hand up.

'Yes, Connor.'

'What time do we meet? And is it here?'

'Yes, it's here,' Steve said. 'And if you could arrive by ten-thirty the day after tomorrow, please. The coach leaves at eleven – on the dot. If you miss the coach, you miss the tournament.'

Tomasz could feel his arms tensing with excitement. This would be his first trip back to Poland since he and his family had left. He had just under two days to wait.

Forty-five and a quarter hours, to be precise.

Tomasz would make sure he was at the coach at least an hour before eleven. Or earlier.

Sunday 13 November
Newcastle 5 United 1
Goals: Yunis
Bookings: Craig, Connor, James

Under-twelves manager's marks out of ten for each player:

Tomasz	5
Connor	5
James	6
Ryan	4
Craig	4
Chi	7
Sam	6
Will	5
Jake	5
Yunis	6
Ben	5

Phoning Home

Tomasz sat staring straight ahead as his dad drove him down the long road that led away from the United Academy. Past the trees. Past the fenced-off football pitches.

The training complex was in an unusual setting. It was in the grounds of a stately home. Beautiful sweeping lawns and a massive, posh – very posh – house. The road Tomasz and his dad were driving along used to be the one that horse-drawn

carriages would take when visiting the owners of the old house.

'You're quiet,' his dad said.

'Am I?' Tomasz said, happy his dad was speaking to him in Polish for once. Usually he insisted they talk English. He wondered why he'd switched.

'Is everything OK?' his dad pressed him.

'Dad, we lost five–one.'

'Yes, I'm sorry,' he said. 'But you

mustn't blame yourself. The defenders were all over the place.'

Tomasz smiled. Not only did his dad know the right thing to say, but he knew about football too. He had always taken an interest in Tomasz's football and came to watch most of his games – even though he was a very busy doctor at the local hospital.

'Do the other boys still tease you?' his dad said, after a pause.

Tomasz stopped smiling. His dad had got to the heart of his worries straight away. He was good at that too.

'A bit,' Tomasz said, trying to sound like he didn't care. But, really, he did care. About Ryan in particular. Ryan was forever having a go. Forever making him feel that he was stupid, just because his English was not perfect. He *wasn't* stupid. He was just mastering the language. He'd like to see Ryan try and make sense in Polish.

'A bit?' his dad said. 'It's more than a bit. I can tell by your voice.'

'I'm OK, Dad. And I'm looking forward to the trip. I can't wait to go back home.'

'England is home, now,' his dad said quietly.

'I know,' Tomasz replied. 'I love it here. But Poland will always be home.'

His dad said nothing.

Tomasz could tell he felt the same.

After tea, the phone rang and Tomasz went to answer it.

'Hello?' Tomasz said.

'Tomasz. It's Leszek. Are you still coming this week?'

Another Polish voice. Tomasz grinned. It was his cousin calling from Lodz.

'Yes,' he said. 'Yes. I can't wait. It'll be good to see you. Are you at home?'

'Yes. Where else?' Leszek said.

Tomasz imagined the house Leszek lived in with his mum and dad, Tomasz's aunt and uncle. It was a house he knew well. It was huge, with a swimming pool and a large back garden with a half-sized goal,

with a net. He and Leszek had grown up together, spending most of their time in that garden, playing with Leszek's older brother, Bogdan.

'So when do you get here?' his cousin asked.

'Tuesday afternoon. Is it still OK if we stay with you?'

'Of course, stupid.'

Tomasz smiled. He hated being made to feel stupid by Ryan, but Leszek could call him stupid all day every day and he wouldn't care.

'And are you and Bogdan coming to all the games? Like we said.'

'Yes. All of them. And if you need an extra player . . .'

Tomasz smiled. He'd love nothing more than to have his cousin in the United team.

After he switched the phone off, Tomasz

At the Airport

Most of the team headed straight for the amusement arcade after they'd made it through passport control at the airport. The others were in an electrical store, looking at gaming consoles and other gadgets.

The boys had nearly an hour to pass until their flight was called for boarding – and they wanted to make the most of it.

Everyone was hyper. Even Steve and the other United coach seemed excited. There were also two parents with them: James's mum and Tomasz's dad. They'd come along to help.

Most of the boys were trying to get away from James's mum, who was constantly asking them if they were OK, suggesting that they shouldn't be drinking so much Coke and telling them to make sure they looked after their bags. It was a bit annoying. Part of the excitement of the trip was being *away* from nagging parents.

However, Steve's words after the Newcastle game rang in the team's ears. *First and foremost, we are representing United.* Everyone knew that they had to behave. Otherwise they'd be sent back home.

Ryan was one of the boys in the amusement arcade. With Ben and Connor.

Ryan felt a bit embarrassed that he – and all the other players – were wearing shirts, smart trousers and jackets, and proper shoes. He looked around at the other boys their age, all off on their holidays. Most of them were wearing jeans, T-shirts and trainers. He wished they could have worn club tracksuits – then everybody would be looking at them.

That's what he liked.

But that wasn't going to happen today.

He glanced over at the electrical shop and saw Tomasz and James coming out of

the shop and heading over to some seats. *Why was James wasting his time with Tomasz?* he thought.

He never quite understood James. He was a mate of Ben's, but was completely unlike him. Ben would have a laugh, have some fun taking the mick out of Tomasz. But not James.

Ryan thought James must be a bit stuck-up. So what if his dad had been an international footballer?

'When's our plane?' Ben said to Connor, breaking Ryan's thoughts.

'It's on the screen,' Connor said. 'Can't you read?'

'Forty minutes,' Ryan cut in before either of them could say anything more.

'I knew that,' Ben said, scowling at Connor.

*

On the other side of the airport lounge, James was asking Tomasz questions.

'What's Poland like, then?'

'Big. Different. There's cities, like here, but countryside too. And it's cold in winter. Much colder than England.'

Tomasz was watching Ryan – with Ben and Connor – as they talked. They looked like they were arguing. Tomasz was glad he was over here.

'And what about the people?'

Tomasz smiled. Sometimes he wanted to say everyone had an extra finger on each hand and Vulcan ears. But he knew that James was genuinely interested in Poland. He was asking the questions as if he really wanted to hear the answers, not trying to set Tomasz up for a joke.

'Nice,' Tomasz said. 'Very nice, mostly.

But there are some people who are not so nice. Like anywhere.'

'And are they into football?'

'Yes. Very. Not just Polish football. German football. And English. There's a lot of City fans and United fans too.'

As James asked more questions, Tomasz felt more and more happy. He was proud. Proud to be taking all his team-mates to Poland.

Back in the amusement arcade, Ryan had run out of pound coins and fifty-pence pieces. He stood by Ben, who was playing on a game shooting guns, not footballs.

Ryan looked over at the adults, the two coaches and two parents, and frowned.

When news about the trip to Poland had come through – and Steve had asked for volunteer helpers – Ryan had asked his mum if she'd come, even though he knew she'd be a pain. She'd phoned Steve straight away. But the team manager had said there was no more room for adults on the trip. There were only four spaces.

Since then, Ryan had wondered if that had been true. Maybe Steve hadn't wanted her to come. He knew the team manager had a problem with his mum.

But right now Ryan really needed her.

Fear of Flying

The plane taxied along the runway, turned slowly and was then ready to take off. The cabin crew had shown them how to grab the oxygen mask from the panel overhead and how to put on the life-jacket in case of a crash. In Polish first, then in English. The Polish version frightened Ryan even more than the English one. For some reason it sounded worse.

But he had still checked the life-jacket was there, secretly slipping his hand

36

underneath his seat. Yes, he could feel it. He knew how to get to it, should he need to.

He'd also read through the emergency instructions card, looking over his shoulder to see where his nearest exit was. And who he'd have to fight to get to the exit first.

Suddenly James's mum leaned over her son, who was sitting next to Ryan.

'Are you all right, Ryan, love? You look a bit nervous. Don't you like flying?'

'I'm fine,' Ryan said in a gruff voice.

'OK, Ryan,' she replied. 'But I'm right here. If you need me.'

Ryan felt embarrassed. James's mum had drawn attention to the fact that he was scared of flying. He saw James eyeing him, still with the emergency instructions in his hands.

'Just checking,' he said, forcing a laugh,

and putting them back in the pouch in the seat in front of him. 'I don't trust these Polish 737s.'

James nodded. He was trying to be supportive to Ryan.

Then the engines fired up. Loud and violent.

This was the bit Ryan dreaded. This was the time he wished his mum was here so he could grab her arm. That's what he'd always done. Every time he'd flown before. But today she wasn't here.

So, instead he had to grip the seat and stare out of the window, pretending he was more relaxed than any of the other boys.

The plane lurched forward and Ryan heard the full-throttle noise that comes as the plane begins to power down the runway.

Behind him, he could hear Tomasz

talking excitedly to his dad. In Polish. Just chatting. Like they weren't about to speed at over 300 miles-an-hour down a length of runway with nothing but fields and houses at the end.

He wondered how Tomasz could possibly be so relaxed. Didn't he know they could all be killed?

The plane was going faster and faster. The noise was terrifying. The rattling of the plane was unbearable. And when he felt the plane lift off, Ryan's stomach lurched. So he closed his eyes. If anyone said something, he could say he was so bored by taking off that he thought he'd go to sleep.

He tried to think about his fantasy: that the manager of Real Madrid under-twelves would see him play and sign him for the Spanish club.

Ryan had heard that planes were most likely to crash in the minute around take-off or the minute around landing. He counted. One to sixty. Then he could relax.

One . . . two . . . three . . .

Then he heard the bang. From underneath the plane. It was as if the plane had hit something – or something had fallen off. He opened his eyes and checked the wing. The jet engine was still there. And he knew . . . he knew that it was the wheels

coming up, knew that the bang was normal.
But he couldn't stop himself thinking
terrible things.

He closed his eyes again.

Four . . . five . . . six . . .

Once they'd been flying a while, James
turned to Ryan.

'My dad's like that,' he said.

'Like what?'

'Afraid of flying. He doesn't like it.'

'I don't mind,' Ryan said, folding his
arms. 'It's boring, that's all. I just wish the
crew would talk in English. And – well – it's
a bit of an old plane. Probably something
the Poles bought off some African country.
It's ancient.'

'So you don't mind flying?' James said,
smiling.

'Nah,' Ryan said. But he could tell

James knew he was lying. But he couldn't say so. Not in front of everyone.

He missed his mum now more than ever. Even though she was always going on at him, he would have liked having her on the plane next to him.

When the cabin crew came along with the drinks trolley he ordered two bottles of Coke and drank the first one swiftly.

Three hours later, Ryan peered out of the window to see fields and hills appearing.

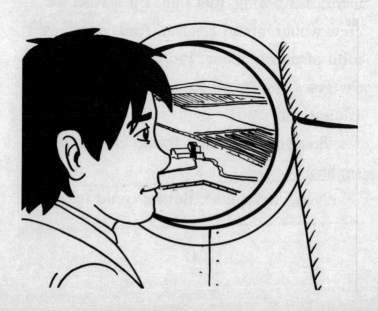

Poland. The plane was descending. And quickly.

He could still hear Tomasz behind him, chattering away. Sometimes in Polish, sometimes in English.

The plane dipped suddenly, too quickly. Ryan gripped both seat arms, brushing James's elbow.

James grinned at Ryan.

Ryan smiled back.

Please don't let the plane crash, he wished, not sure who he was wishing to.

His mind was running through all the things that could happen if the plane didn't land properly. If a wing clipped the runway. If the wheels buckled when they hit the runway. Would the plane smash to pieces? Or would it just land – then burn? He worked out what he'd do in all instances. Then tried to think of other things.

But all he could hear was Tomasz chattering.

I'll be nice to Tomasz, he thought. *If we can just touch down, I'll be nice to Tomasz. I'll stop winding him up.*

Warsaw Airport

Ryan was buzzing when the team
were walking through the airport.
He couldn't stop talking. The plane
hadn't crashed or burned or spun
out of control. He was alive. And he
wanted to make the most of it.

'Look at that. That advert. Is that
Polish, Tomasz?'

Tomasz nodded.

'What's it for?' But Ryan didn't wait for
an answer. 'And why is it in Polish? I

thought they spoke Russian in Poland.'

Tomasz said nothing. Somehow Ryan's digs meant nothing to him now he was back in Poland.

All the signs in Polish made him feel good. So did all the posters advertising things that you couldn't get in England. And hearing all the airport announcements in Polish too. It was great.

Steve led the group through passport control, then customs. Tomasz's dad was there too – counting the boys through, patting each boy on the head as they passed him, saying their name in a firm voice.

There were the usual big signs, some in English, saying ANYTHING TO DECLARE?

'Anything to declare?' Ryan shouted. 'Yeah. Poland stinks.' He held his nose.

'RYAN!'

It was Steve's voice.

Ryan could see that Steve was waiting for him, so he tried to stay at the rear of the group. But Steve dropped back. The other boys and adults were ahead of them now.

Steve walked alongside Ryan. 'I know you're excited. So am I. But I *need* you to set an example for the rest of the boys. You are team captain.'

'Yes, Steve.'

'And what I said, back in England. I meant it. If anyone does anything to attract

bad feeling towards United, I'll be strict. Do you understand?'

'Yes, Steve.'

'That means you could miss a game. Or, worse, be sent home. Get it?'

'Yes, Steve.'

Ryan smiled to himself. There was no way Steve would drop him. He'd have to do something really bad to be out of the team. He was, after all, captain of United's under-twelves.

When Ryan and Steve got to the arrivals hall, at the back of their group, they saw a huge crowd of people. These were the families who had come to collect the boys. Each player was going to spend four days with a Polish family. Each family had a son who played for the Legia Warsaw under-twelves team.

Ryan looked at the families. Inside he felt anxious. He wished he could stay in a hotel. He didn't want to stay with a Polish family. They'd eat weird food, watch foreign TV and he'd have to sit with them and be polite. And none of them would speak English.

Then he heard a roar. Two boys, slightly older than the United players, were running towards them. He wondered if they were the Polish hooligans his mum had warned him about. Until they grabbed Tomasz, slapping him on the back, still shouting. Hugging. Pushing. Tomasz had a massive grin on his face. Ryan couldn't remember seeing Tomasz look so happy.

'My cousins,' he explained to the rest of the group, once he'd escaped from their grip.

Then the cousins went round everyone,

giving them firm handshakes, and saying,
'Welcome to Poland.'

As he was watching, feeling shy and
uncomfortable, Ryan felt a hand on his
shoulder.

What was it now? Did Steve want to tell
him off for something else?

But it was James's mum.

Looking into her face, Ryan actually felt

better – a familiar face amid all this strangeness.

There was a tall blonde woman standing next to James's mum. She was smiling, holding out her hand.

'Ryan,' James's mum said. 'This is your host mother. Mrs Boniek.'

Ryan smiled. 'Hello,' he said, in a voice that surprised him, because it was so quiet.

Faces

The next day the team travelled to
the Legia training ground by coach.
Tomasz noticed a silence among his
team-mates, and he wondered
if they felt about Poland like he had felt
about England when he'd first arrived
there.

He remembered the day very clearly.
Arriving at London's Heathrow airport with
his mum and dad. Knowing that he was
here to stay. And although he'd been to

England before, for holidays and his dad's work trips, England seemed strange this time. First it was the voices: all English. Then it was the huge posters advertising things he'd never seen before: books in English, make-up, cars, banks and some he didn't have a clue what they were advertising.

He had known it would be like this. Moving to a new country must be the strangest thing he'd ever done.

As Tomasz was thinking this, two seats behind him, Ryan was staring out of the coach window.

The first thing Ryan noticed was the people. They looked different in Poland. Ryan remembered seeing Eastern European football teams playing in the Champions League. The people here reminded him of them. Funny looking.

The coach passed through some gates and down a drive that cut its way through what looked like an industrial estate. There were vast warehouses with corrugated-iron sides and enormous signs. In Polish.

No one spoke. Not until the coach stopped and Steve stood up.

All the boys looked up at him. Silent.

'Right, lads,' Steve said. 'This is it.

We've got two hours before kick-off, so I'd like to get out on to the pitch as soon as possible. Lose a bit of the stiffness from all this travelling.'

The doors hissed open and Steve led the team off the coach. They came down the steps in a long line to see groups of people watching them.

Ryan looked around at them all. This was cool. How many times had he seen players coming off coaches on Sky TV?

And now he was doing it, stepping off a coach like a real footballer.

Then suddenly there was a wave of applause. All the people standing around waiting were clapping. Clapping United's under-twelves. Clapping Ryan.

Steve began shaking hands with the people in the crowd as he led the team to the dressing rooms. And Ryan saw James and Ben, Yunis and Jake ahead of him, smiling and shaking hands with people too.

Then a hand came out to Ryan. It was a man: short blond hair, a round red face.

'Welcome to Poland,' the man said.

Ryan shook his hand quickly and walked on with his head down.

The ball swung across the area, high, but dipping. Tomasz raced off his line and was – for a moment – blinded by the sun.

Where was the ball?

He blinked and thrust his arms out where he thought the ball should be. It came into his arms, as if it belonged to him. He pulled the ball to his chest and fell to the ground, shielding it from the Warsaw forwards.

Around him he heard applause and shouts.

'*Brawo* United! *Brawo* United!'

'United! *Hip, hip, hura!*'

Both nice things – in Polish – complimenting him on his goalkeeping.

And at that moment Tomasz felt a huge sense of pride. Here he was, playing football in his home country again. And this time as a United player.

Tomasz got up from making his save and held the ball close to his chest, then bowled it out to Ryan.

Ryan put his foot on it and looked around.

It was hard to make out the other players, there were so many people on the sidelines, all come to see United play Legia Warsaw.

And Ryan knew that among them were players from the other two teams in the tournament too: AC Milan and Real Madrid.

He spotted Jake, ready to make a run down the left, and stroked the ball out to him.

Jake took the ball in his stride, touched it on twice, checked and played the ball across to Yunis.

Jake and Yunis. The Deadly Duo. The source of most of United's goals this season.

Yunis rose to head the ball past the

keeper. But the keeper was ready. Two hands and a chest behind the ball.

Legia were good. This wasn't going to be easy.

Game One

At half-time it was Legia Warsaw 0 United 0.

Ryan felt the game had been even.

But Steve disagreed.

'We've got to get out of our third,' the team manager said, sounding almost angry. 'We're inviting them on to us. Ryan, keep the defence higher up the pitch. Warsaw haven't got much pace. So we can afford to play higher up. And Tomasz?'

Tomasz looked up. He wanted to tell Steve how he'd struggled with the sun. How it'd be easier in the second half. Every time he'd gone for the ball he'd had to cope with the light in his eyes.

'Tomasz,' Steve said. 'You're playing a blinder. If it wasn't for you we'd be three down. And out of the game. You dealt with the sun in your eyes brilliantly.'

Tomasz smiled as Steve went on. 'If we're going to do well in this tournament we need to beat this lot. Milan and Madrid are very strong. Let's take it to them in the second half.'

The second half started with Legia attacking again. But James and Ryan were stopping everything Legia were throwing at them. Legia seemed only to be able to play down the middle. Nothing on the wings.

And United were beginning to grow in confidence.

With twenty minutes to go, James won the ball off Legia again. He shaped to pass it back to Tomasz, then turned and played the ball long across the Legia midfield.

Chi, the team's hard-working midfielder, was on to it.

He trapped it, swivelled, then knocked it back to Sam in deeper midfield. Sam

stroked it hard and wide to Jake, the ball moving without stopping.

That pass alone defeated Legia, because Jake was on to it like a greyhound, beating Legia's right back for pace.

Ryan knew what would happen next. Jake would get close to the edge of the penalty area, then slide the ball into Yunis. Yunis would arrive late, tricking the defender, and score.

Ryan ran into Legia's third of the pitch, ready to pick up the ball if it came loose. Steve had asked him to do this every time United attacked.

Jake took three touches, then played Yunis in. Yunis shot, but the keeper was behind it. However, rather than catch it, the Polish keeper punched the ball out of his box.

Ryan remembered Steve saying that he

should be ready for a punch. Continental keepers punch as much as catch the ball.

It bounced six yards in front of Ryan and Ben. Either of them could have taken the ball. Ben was a better striker, more used to scoring.

But Ryan had spotted that the Legia keeper was still floundering on the ground. So he called for the ball, stepping ahead of Ben, and hit it – like he'd seen a Real Madrid player do the season before. A high ball. Over his team-mates who were expecting a pass. Over the Legia defenders. Over the stranded keeper.

One–nil.

Ryan stood where he'd hit the ball from – thirty yards out at least – and he raised his arms in the air.

Applause surrounded him.

He felt good. Very good.

And he wondered if the Real Madrid under-twelves manager was there. If he'd seen his goal.

After that, the game changed.

Warsaw looked like they'd been punctured. Instead of United playing deep, Warsaw were. Inviting United to attack.

And United accepted the invitation.

Less than ten minutes after his goal, Ryan started another attack. He ran into the space Warsaw had left and played the ball wide to Will on the right. Will took the ball past his first defender and knocked the ball to Yunis. Yunis passed it back to Ryan who'd come further forward. Ryan saw the keeper off his line again.

And he decided: he'd try again.

He was good at this.

He chipped the ball. But instead of

floating over the keeper's head and into the
net, as he'd expected, the ball screwed to
the left and fell well short of the goal. But
still in the penalty area – to where Will had
run, marked closely by a Polish defender.

Will leaped above the defender and
glanced the ball over him. And over the
keeper.

Two–nil.

Ryan stood again – his arms in the air.

To more applause.

One Down, Two to Go

'Were we brilliant or were they rubbish?' Ryan said, holding his hand up.

The boys were back in the dressing rooms. The game over. Four–nil.

Ben high-fived Ryan. Then James. Then Connor.

'Awesome,' Ryan said. 'Who's next?'

'Milan,' James said in a serious voice.

'Milan?'

'It might not be as easy against Milan,' James said.

Ryan nodded quickly. He was buzzing. *Really* excited after the game. And his goal. But he didn't want to be worrying about the next game. He wanted to feel good about this one.

'Well, no one's going to be as easy as that lot,' Ryan said. 'Polish keepers, eh? Rubbish.'

Tomasz, sitting on one of the dressing-room benches, glanced up at Ryan.

'Present company excepted,' Ryan said quickly.

'If it wasn't for Polish keepers,' a voice behind them said, 'then *we* could have been sitting here having been stuffed four–nil.'

It was Steve. He'd just come into the room.

'Yeah,' Ryan said. 'Well played, Tomasz.'

Tomasz was feeling funny. He accepted that he'd had a big part in the victory. Especially in the first half. And he was thrilled to have kept a clean sheet against the Polish team. But – once again – Ryan was getting to him. Everything he said seemed to be loaded with the idea that anything Polish was rubbish.

A small part of him wished that Legia had beaten them. Just to prove a point.

Steve came up to Tomasz. He put his hand on his back and crouched next to him.

'Well played, Tomasz. I bet your dad is a proud man out there, telling everybody about his son.'

Tomasz grinned.

Steve stood up.

'Ryan?'

'Yes, Steve?'

'You played well. Good captaincy. Good goal. And you really helped take the game to them.' Steve glanced at the door, then spoke in a quieter voice. 'Can I have a word with you outside?'

'Sure, Steve,' Ryan said, bouncing out of the room.

What was this about? Was Steve going
to give him something?

Then it occurred to him. Maybe
someone from Real Madrid *had* seen
him play. Maybe they wanted to talk to
him?

Steve led Ryan along a corridor,
through a door and into what looked like
someone else's office. There were posters
on the wall. One with all the muscles of
the body laid bare.

'How are you getting on, Ryan?' Steve
said, breaking Ryan's train of thought.

'Good,' Ryan said. 'Great.'

'What about your host family? Are they
looking after you?'

'Yeah. It's OK, I suppose.' He thought
about the tall blonde woman. She'd been
kind. Very kind. He even had an en-suite
room, so he didn't have to walk about in

the house when he needed the toilet. The son was OK. But he barely spoke any English. And anyway, he was only a Legia Warsaw player. It's not like he was Real or Milan.

'OK?' Steve said. 'What do you mean?'

'Well, you know. They take some understanding. The mum speaks decent English. But the rest of them . . .'

Steve nodded.

'And the food's a bit weird,' Ryan went on. 'You know, funny tasting . . .'

Steve put his hand up.

Ryan stopped talking.

'Ryan. You do realize this is *Poland. Not* England. That people don't speak English as a first language on the whole. That they don't eat English food: they eat what they like and have liked for hundreds of years.

And that – if anything – *you* should be speaking to them in *Polish*.'

Ryan laughed. 'But everyone should speak English. Don't they learn it?'

'Some do,' Steve said. 'Listen. This isn't a telling off. Just a quiet word. But remember what I said about respect. Respecting Poland. We *are* their guests.'

Ryan stopped smiling. 'I'm sorry,' he said.

'OK,' Steve said. 'Anything else? Are the rest of the boys happy? I look to you to keep an eye out for all of them.'

'Yeah, Steve. They're fine.'

'Good, Ryan,' Steve said. 'Well, let me know if anything comes up.'

'I will.'

'OK,' Steve said. 'Now let's go and watch the other match. I bet you're looking forward to seeing Real.'

And Steve and Ryan walked back down
the corridor to join the rest of the team.

Wednesday 16 November
Legia Warsaw 0 United 4
Goals: Ryan, Will, Yunis, Jake
Bookings: Chi, Sam

Under-twelves manager's marks out of ten for each player:

Tomasz	8
Connor	7
James	8
Ryan	8
Craig	6
Chi	6
Sam	7
Will	7
Jake	8
Yunis	8
Ben	8

Real v Milan

Ryan joined his team-mates on the sidelines to watch Real Madrid under-twelves play AC Milan under-twelves.

He stood next to James and Ben.

'They're good,' James said, in his usual quiet but assured voice.

Ryan could *see* that Madrid and Milan were good. Madrid especially. They were passing the ball around with ease.

One touch. Pass. One touch. Pass.

Ryan wondered how United would be able to defend against this sort of football. It was like watching Real Madrid's first team. Not their kids.

But he was interested to see that the players were not all giants like the Legia Warsaw players had been. Some of them were tiny, smaller than Jake. But once they were on the ball, they seemed to be able to do anything with it.

Although it was going to be hard, Ryan couldn't wait to play against Real Madrid. It was his dream. One of the things he'd really been looking forward to.

The second game of the tournament ended Real Madrid 2 AC Milan 2.

Both teams were applauded off the pitch by the mostly Polish crowd.

The tournament was under way.

The format of the four-team tournament was simple. All teams had to play each other once. A game a day. Three games each. Then the top two teams would play in a final on the last day – to win the Tomasz Milosz trophy.

After each team had played once, the tournament table looked like this:

	Played	Won	Drawn	Lost	For–Against	Points
United	1	1	0	0	4–0	3
Real	1	0	1	0	2–2	1
Milan	1	0	1	0	2–2	1
Legia	1	0	0	1	0–4	0

A good start for United. A very good start.

After the Spanish and Italian players were changed, there was an evening welcome party for the players of all four teams at the

Legia stadium – in a banqueting suite that overlooked the pitch.

Tomasz was very happy. That he was here. Part of the tournament. And that he had come back to Poland wearing an English football shirt. United's. One of the most famous shirts in the world.

During the party there'd been a series of speeches, in Polish, Italian, Spanish and English. Just beforehand, Tomasz talked to a Legia Warsaw player called Lukasz. He found out he was from the same part of

town as he was. As they talked, Tomasz felt some of his local accent coming back. It was a nice feeling.

Tomasz watched everyone during the speeches.

Ryan rolled his eyes at all the different languages.

The Real players, clustered together, wearing ties and blazers, listening in silence.

The Legia players, all wearing team tracksuits, some of them talking during the Italian version of the speech.

The Italians, all dark hair and confident smiles, even though they'd drawn their opening game.

And then Tomasz looked at his team-mates. His *English* team-mates. He saw Jake and Yunis standing together, shoulder to shoulder, even if Jake was a foot shorter. And James and Ben, the only two black lads in the room, drinking Coke from their glasses at exactly the same time. Even Ryan, who gave him so much trouble. These were his team-mates. He was one of them. A United player: not a Polish player. An *English* player. He felt proud to be among them.

But then – out of the corner of his eye – he saw a group of other boys standing near James and Ben. Polish boys. All wearing the same kind of jacket – black leather. They definitely weren't Legia players, he'd have recognized them. Maybe they were supporters from the games earlier, Tomasz thought. They must have been something to do with *someone* – or they wouldn't be at the reception.

Tomasz wasn't quite sure what was going on, but he saw one of them laugh, then push James on purpose. Only gently. But it was a push all the same.

James turned round. He'd spilled his drink down his front, but he looked at the boys in a friendly way.

He thinks it was an accident, Tomasz thought.

Then he saw the lads hold their hands up – as if to say it *had* been an accident.

Tomasz didn't like what he'd seen. Why had they done that? Pushed James on purpose. Because he was sure they had done it deliberately. There was something about it all that worried him.

Hero

The party was nearly over when Tomasz heard a knocking on a microphone.

Someone was going to make a speech. Another speech! Even Tomasz was tired of hearing everything in four languages. He looked at his dad, as if to say *This is getting boring*. But his dad was staring at the stage, his eyes as big as footballs.

Tomasz glanced at the stage. A tall man – in his sixties – was standing, waiting to be introduced. A man with *enormous* hands. Who was he, that his dad would be so interested?

'Ladies and gentlemen,' the host of the evening said. 'We are delighted that a special guest has been able to join us this evening. He was not meant to be coming until the final day of the tournament, but here he is. I give you Tomasz Milosz.'

Tomasz's jaw dropped.

Here was his dad's hero. The former Poland goalkeeper. The player he'd been named after.

'I am very happy to be here,' Milosz said in English. 'To witness this excellent tournament – and to have it named after me. Thank you.'

Milosz paused. Some of the audience thought he had finished and began to clap.

But the keeper held one of his giant hands up. 'No, I have not finished,' he said, laughing. 'I have more to say. That it is good to see teams from four of the best footballing countries in the world – England, Spain and Italy – and Poland!'

The audience laughed as one.

'Especially England,' he said. 'I want to congratulate the English team – United – for being top of the league table so far. You beat Legia well.'

The crowd groaned.

'But you never know,' Milosz said. 'As some of you may remember, in 1973 I was called The Clown by the English. But that day I had the last laugh when Poland beat England. But today England had the last laugh.'

The goalkeeper paused again.

'Maybe Legia will play United in the final. Who will have the last laugh then?'

The audience began to applaud.

'Thank you,' Milosz said. 'That really is the end of my speech. Enjoy your tournament, boys.'

After the speech, Tomasz went over to his dad.

'Has he gone?'

'I think so,' Tomasz's dad said. 'Maybe we'll meet him later.'

His dad was grinning like a child.

'I hope so,' Tomasz said. 'I hope so.' Something about talking to a man who used to keep goal for Poland excited him in a way he had never felt before.

Home from Home

This was the second time Ryan had gone home with his host family.

On the first night he had pretended to be tired and gone to bed. The next morning he'd come down late, avoiding the father of the house, who he had yet to meet.

He actually quite liked his host mum. She spoke perfect English and was very gentle and kind.

She drove him home. The car was a

large jeep, almost as big as a Humvee. Ryan thought that they must be loaded.

The boy – Lech – who'd not played for Legia that day, as he was injured, was asking Ryan questions, his mum translating.

Ryan couldn't work out what Lech wanted to say. He felt a bit stupid, being unable to talk the language the other people in the car were speaking.

'Lech wants to know what it's like to play for United. And do you know the first-team players?'

Ryan nodded. 'I've met a few,' he said, still not feeling like talking. But at least now he could talk about himself. 'And it's good playing for United. Sometimes we get to go to first-team games. If there's space.'

The mum relayed this information back

to Lech in Polish. The boy nodded and seemed very excited.

His mum spoke next. 'Lech is a big fan of your United. He watches them on television here in Poland.'

Ryan nodded.

There was a silence. He knew he should ask a question now, show an interest in them and not just talk about himself.

'How long has Lech been a Legia Warsaw player?' Ryan asked.

The mum asked Lech the question in Polish.

The boy held his hand up. Three fingers.

Ryan nodded. 'I have been at United for four,' he said.

He held up four fingers.

Lech nodded, smiled and said something else.

'My son says he has some DVDs of United, and would you like to watch them with him tonight?'

'Yes,' Ryan said. '*Da*.'

Suddenly he felt better. He had been uneasy about having a meal with his host family tonight. But now maybe it would be OK.

He smiled as the big four-wheel-drive passed through the suburbs of Warsaw to their home.

Phoning England

Ryan smiled at his host mum, and started to dial. First the UK code, then his home number – without the zero at the start.

Mrs Boniek had shown him what to do. She was nice.

After a click, the phone began to ring.

Ryan looked around the room. It was a small living room. Everything was neat and tidy, apart from two piles of books on the floor.

'Yeah?' It was Ryan's mum.

'Hello, Mum. It's me.'

'Ryan? Are you OK? Did you win your match?'

Ryan knew his mum would know they'd played today. She'd have been worrying about the game.

'Yeah. Four–nil.'

'Brilliant. I bet they were rubbish,' his mum said. 'You were playing the Poles first, weren't you?'

'Yeah.' Ryan wanted to tell his mum about his goal. But he couldn't get a word in.

'Mum?'

'It'll be harder against the others, Ryan. You know that. Eastern European football is nothing compared to football in Italy and Spain.'

Ryan said nothing. There was no point. Once his mum got going.

'They'll be passing it about. You'll be lucky to get a touch.' And off she went, talking about teams she'd never seen, and never would do, because she wasn't here.

After a pause, his mum said, 'And what are the family like you're staying with? Are they looking after you? Because if they're not I'll phone Steve and sort him out.'

'They're fine,' Ryan said.

'Have they given you food?'

'Not yet. I've been –'

'Not yet? You've been there a day already.'

'I meant tonight. We ate at –'

'I'm going to phone Steve. I knew they wouldn't look after you. Why should they? They don't know you from Adam . . .'

'Mum!' Ryan said. 'They're nice. The mum has been really kind. She showed me how to use the phone. She's offered me loads of food.'

'Oh she has, has she?'

Ryan stared at the ceiling. He knew what was coming next. Why couldn't his mum be normal like other mums?

'So you'd like to stay over there?' his mum said. 'Don't I look after you well enough?'

'Mum, I –'

'What's she offered you to eat?'

'I dunno. Bread –'

'Bread. Is that it?'

'Mum –'

'What sort of bread?'

'Mum,' Ryan shouted. 'I scored today . . .'

Milan

The following day, Tomasz was warming up just before the Milan game. Stretching each leg. His thighs. His calves. His ankles. Then moving to his shoulders. Warming them up. Pushing them as far as they could go.

It was a fine morning. Warmer than the day before.

Then he saw Lukasz running over to him, looking like something was wrong. He hoped everything was all right. He'd got on well with the Legia player at the after-match party the night before.

'Everything OK?' Tomasz said.

'Yes. It's OK,' Lukasz said. 'But have you seen who's here?'

'Who? Tomasz Milosz?' Tomasz was excited at the thought of playing in front of the former Poland keeper.

'Not just him. Robert Dejna from the Polish national youth squad too.'

'But your game with Real isn't for a couple of hours, is it?'

Tomasz was assuming that the Polish coach would not be interested in watching the English and Italian teams.

'Exactly,' said Lukasz.

'What?'

'He's come early.'

'So?'

'So?' Lucasz said. 'He's come to see you.'

At first Tomasz had been excited. A Poland international coach was scouting him. He had never even dreamed that he could one day play for Poland.

But now, standing in the goal, with six Italian boys up for a corner kick, he felt nervous.

The hardest thing for him was that he had never before felt like he was being judged. He just played. But now, he was

aware he was being looked at so closely, that he couldn't concentrate.

Looking for the scout again, he saw the four boys from the reception. The ones who had pushed James. All in matching jackets.

Then he heard his name being called out. A team-mate. The corner had been taken – while he was staring at the side of the pitch.

As the ball swung across from the corner flag, Tomasz hesitated.

And that was the thing. He *never* hesitated. He was off his game – big time.

Luckily James rose to head the ball behind for another corner.

Then Tomasz heard Ryan's voice.

'Tomasz. What's going on? Call for it.'

Tomasz nodded. Ryan was right. He *should* have called for it, then caught it, even punched it. Ryan was the team captain. It was his job to say things like that.

Tomasz looked across at the crowd on the side of the pitch. He wanted to work out which was the scout for the Polish international team. Had he noticed his mistake?

The game was hard. Milan were all over United. The Italian players were clearly much better at passing the ball.

The first incident involved Craig. Craig was the team's hothead. He'd already been sent off once this season. Trying to keep up with a speedy Italian winger, Craig was losing ground. So he slid in a low tackle. The ball was long gone when he took the player down. The player dived and rolled over four times before clutching his leg, his eyes fixed on the referee.

The referee waved the Italian physio on, then went for his pocket to pull out a card. Tomasz watched. He was convinced the card would be red. The referee looked so sure of himself.

He saw Craig stand with his hands on hips, looking at the card.

Yellow.

And then the Italians surrounded the referee. *Trying to get Craig sent off*, Tomasz thought.

After that, the Italian team was even better. Their anger spurred them on.

United managed to keep them out only because of hard work and never giving up.

Until just before half-time.

With a minute to go before the break, a Milan player beat the United defence and was suddenly one-on-one with Tomasz. Ryan was the closest defender and he was forced to tackle the Italian in the penalty area.

The Italian went down. But Ryan knew he'd got the ball.

Then the referee blew his whistle – and pointed at the spot.

Ryan was on his feet. 'The ball,' he shouted at the referee. 'I got the ball.'

'Penalty,' the referee said in a calm voice.

'No way!' Ryan thrust his arms out.

And, not meaning to, he caught the referee's arm.

Out came another yellow card.

United were losing it.

And from the minute Tomasz had to pick the ball out of the net after the penalty had been scored, he knew that Ryan was in the foulest of Ryan-moods imaginable.

Punched

Late in the game – with the score still AC Milan 1 United 0 – a corner kick came low over the penalty area. It should have been an easy catch for a keeper, but Tomasz had been looking for the Poland coach again. He knew he shouldn't be, but he couldn't help it. The idea that he was watching the game was too distracting.

When he realized that the ball was coming over, Tomasz lunged off his line.

But he was too late. With so many players in the way, there was no chance he could catch it. So he went to punch it.

Even though he knew he was no good at punching.

Reaching for the ball with his fist, he felt it slip down the side of his glove as he fell to the ground over another player. He was worried he'd given a penalty away, pushing the player over. But was relieved to see that he was on top of another United player.

Get to your feet. That was the first thing he knew he had to do. So he stood and faced where he thought the ball had gone. And there was a tall Italian – in red and black stripes – side-footing the ball into the net.

Two–nil.

'Why did you punch it?' the player Tomasz had flattened was shouting.

It was Ryan!

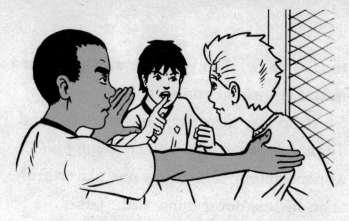

'I couldn't –'

Ryan didn't let him finish. 'You were looking over there. Who are you looking for?'

Ryan was still angry about conceding the penalty. But now he was angry about this as well.

Tomasz blushed a fierce red. Ryan was right. He'd not been concentrating. Too busy looking for the Polish coach.

He'd let everyone down.

But then Tomasz felt James's arm round him.

James held up his hand to Ryan. 'Come on, Ryan. One mistake. Tomasz kept us in the last game. And you gave away their first goal. Let's just get on with it.'

Ryan was silent for a few seconds. And Tomasz knew that he was choosing his words carefully. There was one player in the team he was never funny with: James.

'He's not concentrating, James,' Ryan said eventually. 'That's Polish keepers for you. They're rubbish. He's a clown. Like that Tomaszsoandso at the party yesterday. And I did *not* give away the first goal. I got the ball.'

'Leave it, Ryan,' James said. 'We've got a game to play.'

So Ryan left it.

But as soon as the game was over – and as soon as he could get Tomasz on his own – Ryan laid into him.

'You blew it,' Ryan shouted. 'Two–nil. We lost two–nil.'

Tomasz usually put up with Ryan attacking him – and the things he said about him and Poland. But today *he* was angry too. He'd just blown it in front of the Poland international youth coach. He'd had enough.

So he attacked back.

'You gave away the first goal. Why is it all my fault?'

Then Ryan pushed him. Not hard. But it was a push all the same.

'I got the ball,' Ryan shouted. 'It wasn't my fault. But you daydreaming *was* your fault.'

Neither of them saw the figure running across the fields towards them, coming fast and silent over the grass.

'I'm sick of you,' Tomasz spat out.

'I'm sick of you,' Ryan mimicked in what he thought was a funny Polish accent.

Tomasz closed his eyes. Then opened

them again. 'You think it's a joke to be Polish. Better to be English?'

'Erm . . . yes.' Ryan was grinning.

Tomasz was furious. He hated this in Ryan. How he kept criticizing him and his country. So he breathed in and said it. It didn't matter what Ryan did back.

'You didn't get the ball. You took the player and you gave away a penalty. *You* lost the game for us.'

That's when Ryan hit Tomasz.

Then he jumped on top of him, holding him down.

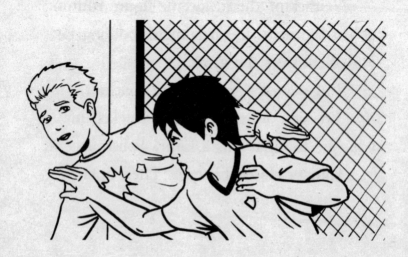

'I never lose us the games,' he shouted.
'I win us the games. You lost it. You and
your stupid Polish punching-of-the-ball. On
this stupid Polish football field. With all its
clown goalkeepers. And clown people with
their funny faces and –'

Ryan felt himself being pulled skywards.

The man running across the fields had
reached them. He put Ryan on his feet,
glared at him, then checked to see if
Tomasz was OK.

Steve!

Steve looked at Ryan. 'Go and get
changed. Then wait for me. Do not join
the other teams having lunch. Understand?'
He said all this in a quiet controlled
voice that meant one thing. Trouble. Big
trouble.

'Yes, Steve,' Ryan said.

And Tomasz heard the sobs in his voice.

Thursday 17 November
AC Milan 2 United 0
Goals: none
Bookings: Craig, Ryan

Under-twelves manager's marks out of ten for each player:

Tomasz	6
Connor	5
James	7
Ryan	4
Craig	5
Chi	6
Sam	5
Will	6
Jake	6
Yunis	6
Ben	6

Banned

Steve came into the empty dressing room. All the other players had gone to the lunch that Legia Warsaw had put on for all the teams.

'Sit down, Ryan.'

Ryan sat on the bench, looking around at the mud streaks on the floor, the pale white walls and pegs without any kitbags hanging on them.

Steve said nothing for a few seconds.

Ryan looked back at him.

This, he realized, was worse than being shouted at. Silence. He was used to being shouted at, bawled at, yelled at by his mum. But Steve's silence and grim stare were too much.

A part of him felt like crying. But he would not cry. He never cried. Not since the day his dad had left his mum. He was the man of the house now. His little brothers might cry, but he didn't.

'Ryan?'

'Yes, Steve.'

'Have you anything to say?'

'I'm sorry. I'm really sorry. I shouldn't have hit Tomasz.'

'Anything else?'

Ryan's mind froze. He could think of nothing else.

So Steve breathed in. A long breath.

Ryan wondered what he had to say

that he'd need so much breath to say it
with.

'I am cross about you hitting Tomasz,
yes. But I am more cross about the things I
heard you saying to him. What do you think
you said that was wrong?'

Ryan said nothing. But he knew Steve
would wait a long time for an answer. So he
said, in a quiet voice, 'About Poland?'

'Yes, Ryan. About Poland. And it's not
just what you said then. I heard you saying
things on the pitch. And you were saying
things on the way over here in the plane.

115

And even back at the Academy.' Steve paused. 'I am very disappointed in you.'

Ryan hung his head. If there was anyone in the world he didn't want to hear that from, it was Steve.

'I'm sorry,' Ryan said again.

'I'm sure you are. I believe you. But this is not the first time this has happened, is it? Remember the start of this season. When you bullied Jake?'

Ryan remained silent.

'I have made a decision that I didn't want to have to make,' Steve said.

Ryan watched Steve. He knew this was where the conversation was going. His punishment. But what was it going to be?

Ryan thought he already knew.

'I am taking the captaincy off you when we get home,' Steve said. 'I don't think you are ready to be a leader.'

That was exactly what Ryan had thought he would say. And, in a funny way, it was a relief to him. At least he was still a United player. It could have been worse. Steve had not released him or anything like that. Nor had he sent Ryan home. Then he would have missed the next game against Real Madrid. The one he really wanted to play in.

'And there's something else.'

Ryan frowned. Steve saw it.

'Don't worry. I'm not going to send you home.'

Ryan sighed. It was a relief. A huge relief.

'And do you want to know why I'm not sending you home?'

Ryan didn't know what to answer. He stared at Steve. He didn't know what to think.

'Because Tomasz said that the fight was half his fault.'

Ryan looked surprised. But he still said nothing. *So, Tomasz had stuck up for him.*

'But I am,' Steve went on, 'going to ban you for one game.'

Ryan nodded. So, he'd miss a game when they were back home. So what?

'Tomorrow's game,' Steve said.

Ryan looked at him. 'But tomorrow . . .'

'Is Real Madrid.'

'But I . . .'

'You want to play against Real Madrid. I know.'

'Please . . .'

Ryan heard the word 'please' come from his mouth. It sounded weak and high pitched. And then he felt a weight on his eyelids. A swelling. For a second he was confused. Then, as tears streamed down his face, he realized that, for the first time in years, he was crying.

	Played	Won	Drawn	Lost	For–Against	Points
Milan	2	1	1	0	4–2	4
United	2	1	0	1	4–2	3
Legia	2	1	0	1	3–6	3
Real	2	0	1	1	4–5	1

The Clown

Tomasz had watched Steve send Ryan off after the game. And part of him was glad that his team manager was going to do something. Ryan was a bully. Everyone knew it. And someone had to do something about it.

But another part of him felt guilty. Very guilty.

He asked himself a question: Why had Ryan had a go at him?

What was the answer?

Because he'd made a mess of the second goal.

And whose fault was it?

His own. Not Ryan's. He had lost concentration. He'd been looking for the Polish scout.

Ryan had been right to be so cross. Maybe Tomasz *had* lost them the game.

Wanting to be on his own after the game, he was hanging around the pitch until the two teams of boys had gone back to the dressing rooms. He was doing what he always did when he had spare time on a pitch: throwing the ball against the post, then testing his reflexes as the ball came back at him. Either to his left, his right, or straight at him.

'I used to do that.'

Tomasz caught the ball. Had someone just spoken? He froze, still wanting to be alone.

'I said that I used to do that.'

Tomasz turned round. And there, huge in a suit and tie, was Tomasz Milosz. *The* Tomasz Milosz.

Tomasz said nothing. He was dumbstruck.

The former Polish international keeper put his hand out. It was huge. A real goalkeeper's hand.

Tomasz took it. His own hand looked like a baby's in comparison.

'Hello,' was all he could think to say.

Because here he was facing one of Poland's greatest footballers. Although he'd never seen him play, he'd heard about him again and again from his dad. And seen footage of him on TV.

'You had a tough game today,' Milosz said.

Tomasz nodded.

'But you shouldn't be too hard on yourself. Except for that one mistake, you've been excellent. I saw your game against Legia too. You were outstanding.'

Tomasz blushed. He hadn't known that. And suddenly he felt a whole lot better.

'Thank you,' Tomasz said in a quiet voice.

Milosz went on. 'What I'm saying is . . . try to remember *all* the games you play. Not one second of one game today. Overall you have made twenty or thirty good decisions in this tournament. One bad one. That makes you a very good keeper in my opinion.'

Tomasz smiled and nodded. He wished his dad was with him to hear this and not back in the club rooms. It would make him so proud.

Milosz shook Tomasz's hand again. 'I'll see you at your next game. Tomorrow. Against Madrid?'

'Yes,' Tomasz said. 'Real Madrid.'

'Well, good luck.'

Milosz made to go. But Tomasz called out to him. There was something he wanted to know.

'Can I ask you a question?'

'Of course.'

'Did you mind being called The Clown?'

The former keeper smiled.

'The English called me a clown *before* the game against England,' Milosz said. 'It made me play better. It helped Poland draw with England. So, no, I didn't mind.'

Tomasz beamed. That was it. Being called a clown – or anything – by Ryan wouldn't get to him any more. It would only make him stronger, more determined to prove him wrong.

Unreal

Ryan sat on the sidelines, watching.
He could clearly remember the
last time he'd sat out a game. When
he was injured a couple of seasons ago.
United under-tens against City under-tens.
They'd lost the match without him. And
he'd hated it.

It was torture watching his team play –
being able to do nothing to help them. But
this was worse than that day. Far worse.

Because *this* game was against Real
Madrid.

It was also torture watching Tony play
in his place.

Ryan had loved Real for years. He'd first
seen them when his dad was still at home
and they'd had Sky Sports One. They had
the full sports package then. And his dad
used to let him stay up to watch Spanish

games at the weekend. Once he'd seen Real playing, passing the ball and scoring such wonderful goals, he'd been hooked.

Last Christmas, his dad had got Ryan a Real top. He'd worn it for a week – including in bed. It was still his favourite one.

And now he was watching Real Madrid under-twelves. Watching them, not playing against them. And like every Real side he'd seen, they were brilliant at passing the ball around.

Ten, fifteen passes per move.

United only needed a draw against Real Madrid to reach the final. Warsaw had beaten Milan three–two in the match that morning. If United *did* draw, then they'd finish above Milan on goal difference – to play Legia Warsaw in the final.

But Ryan could tell that wasn't going to

happen. Every time Madrid attacked they looked like scoring.

And yet United *were* defending well. James was running the defence perfectly. They were playing as a unit, making it impossible for Real to get behind them. All Real could do was shoot from distance. And none of their shots troubled Tomasz.

But United had no chance to attack.

In the second half United began to look tired. And Real Madrid started to take advantage.

In one attack, the Real winger, who was even faster than Jake, took the ball to the corner and crossed it. The ball skimmed over heads, reaching the Spanish team's tall striker, who headed it to the bottom right corner of United's goal.

Ryan winced. It was a goal, surely.

But somehow Tomasz got to it. He'd dived low and tipped the ball around the post for a corner kick.

Ryan was amazed.

Real had another corner.

The ball went flying hard into the penalty area. Tomasz came off his line and leaped at the ball.

Ryan closed his eyes, hoping Tomasz would not try to punch it again. But when he opened his eyes, Tomasz was lying on the ground holding the ball, the whole crowd applauding.

But still Real came at them.

Wave after wave of white shirts.

And even though Ben had one chance cleared off the line, Ryan was worried that it was just a matter of time before Madrid scored.

And just into injury time, ninety minutes

gone, it became inevitable. James, who had made so many tackles to resist Madrid, mistimed one in the penalty area, chopping a player down.

The referee had no option: he blew his whistle and pointed to the spot.

Penalty.

It was the big striker against Tomasz.

The striker placed the ball on the spot.

Tomasz took his place on the line.

Ryan could see him moving from foot to foot. He'd noticed him do that before.

When the referee blew his whistle, the crowd went silent. So silent you could hear the birds singing in the trees around the ground.

Then Ryan saw Tomasz look over at his two cousins who were watching the game. The ones who had met him at the airport. Then he caught Ryan's eye. Just for a second. And Ryan wondered what Tomasz had been thinking. He wished he'd given him a thumbs up, or something. To give him confidence.

But there hadn't been time. Because the striker was stepping up to the ball.

Tomasz shifted his weight on to his left foot, then his right. Eyes on the striker.

The striker hit the ball, hard and high to the left.

Tomasz leaped. The right way. But the ball was travelling too fast. He would never reach it.

Tomasz flailed in the air, the ball skimming past his gloved hand. But somehow he got a fingertip on to the ball and it moved slightly in the air, smacking against the post, ricocheting back into the penalty area.

To the Spanish winger. The one with the pace.

The winger hit it hard into the open goal, Tomasz on the floor.

Except he wasn't on the ground. He was somehow standing at the centre of his goal, taking the ball with both hands, holding it close to his stomach.

Then the wild applause – from everybody, including Ryan – as the referee blew for full-time.

	Played	Won	Drawn	Lost	For–Against	Points
Legia	3	2	0	1	6–8	6
United	3	1	1	1	4–2	4
Milan	3	1	1	1	6–5	4
Real	3	0	2	1	4–5	2

Friday 18 November
Real Madrid 0 United 0
Goals: none
Bookings: none

Under-twelves manager's marks out of ten for each player:

Tomasz	9
Connor	7
James	8
Tony	6
Craig	7
Chi	8
Sam	7
Will	6
Jake	6
Yunis	6
Ben	7

Attack

Tomasz was mobbed by the rest of the team after the game. James put his arm round him and walked him all the way back from the pitch, Ben alongside them, beaming.

They had qualified for the final.

'You saved me,' James said. 'I thought I'd blown it.'

'You're joking,' Tomasz said. 'You saved us. How many times did you tackle one of their players when they would have been through on goal?'

'Yeah, but I gave away the penalty that could have lost us the game,' James said.

Tomasz thought about what Milosz had said to him the day before. *Try to remember* all *the games you play. Not one second of one game.*

'We'd have been three or four down if you hadn't made those tackles. You saved the game. Forget the one mistake you made. Think of all the good tackles.'

Tomasz saw James nodding. The three of them – Tomasz, James and Ben – walked on in silence. All grinning.

And that was when Tomasz noticed the four lads again – from the party after the first game. The ones who had pushed James and he'd spilled his drink. The ones in the matching jackets. All looking angry. All staring at James and Ben.

Ryan didn't know what to do after the game. He wanted to go into the dressing room and congratulate his team-mates. But he felt a bit separate from them today. Because he hadn't played.

James's mum had asked him to give James a message: that she'd gone back to the hotel to fetch something. But still Ryan felt uneasy going in to see the others. So he waited on the other side of the car park among the parents and the coaches and the other fans. Including Tomasz's two cousins and the four lads he'd seen watching the game.

It wasn't long before some of the players emerged. James and Ben were out first. They walked outside, James pulling out a mobile phone.

Ryan thought, *He's going to phone his dad. Tell him we got to the final.*

But then something strange happened.

The four Polish lads went up to James and Ben. And, before Ryan knew what was happening, one of them pushed Ben.

James pushed another of them back.

Then one of the four hit James.

Hard.

So hard he fell down and cried out.

Ryan felt paralysed as he saw all this. As

if he was watching it on TV. He felt he could do nothing. Then he saw Tomasz come out of the dressing room to see what was happening.

Tomasz shouted something in Polish to his cousins and ran over to James and Ben.

He stood between James and Ben and the four lads.

The lads pushed Tomasz too, but stepped back when his cousins arrived.

There was a stand-off, James back on his feet, until the four lads turned and ran away, disappearing before any adults could confront them.

Ryan stayed where he was as everything calmed down. He was feeling confused and upset. Should he have gone over and helped? Would it have made any difference?

He saw Steve come out, reacting quickly. Gesturing to the Polish team coaches, who immediately made calls on their mobile phones. Phoning the police, Ryan assumed.

Finally, Ryan saw Tomasz's dad come out and sit James down on a bench. Tomasz's dad looked at James's face, then took some sort of wipe out of his bag. He cleaned James's wound and put a plaster over it.

Ryan remembered that Tomasz's dad was a doctor back in England. That was why he was helping James. He knew what to do. And it made Ryan think about Tomasz as well: he'd known what to do too. He'd stood up to the four bullies – to protect his friend.

Last Night

It was the last night the team would
spend in Poland. Although United had
got through to the final the following
lunchtime, they would fly home straight
afterwards, in the evening.

Steve had got the boys together in a
restaurant in the centre of Warsaw, near the
Legia training grounds. Tonight was to be the
celebration of their time together in Poland,
and Steve would top it off by announcing the
player of the tournament award.

All the United players were there along with their host families and Tomasz's cousins.

James's mother was talking to all the boys, topping up their water, making sure they had their napkins on their knees. At the start of the trip, some of the boys had found her annoying, but now they did what she asked and actually quite liked having her there.

They were all seated at three long

tables, arranged in a horseshoe shape. Steve sat at the tables' head.

After the toasts – to Legia Warsaw, and the host families – and before the award announcement, Steve stood up.

'I wanted to get something out of the way before we eat,' he said. 'I won't say much, but I must say something.'

Everyone knew what he was talking about. The attack on James and Ben.

Ryan looked down at his plate: still guilty he'd done nothing to help.

'As you know,' Steve said, 'there was a bit of trouble earlier today. A group of young lads picked on James and Ben. And as you can *see*, James is sitting next to me. Ben next to him. They're both OK, aren't you, lads?'

Ben and James nodded.

'If it wasn't for the quick thinking of

Tomasz – and the support of his cousins –
it would have been a lot worse. So I'd like
to ask you all to raise your glasses to
Tomasz and his cousins.'

The people round the table stood, raised
their glasses and broke out into applause.

Once everyone had sat down, Steve
began again.

'Despite this incident, we have had a
great time here. The people of Warsaw, the
club, the families we have been staying with,
have been welcoming and generous. The
youths who we came across today decided to
pick on James and Ben because they were
different from themselves. I think this is a
lesson to everyone that, although we have
different languages, different-coloured skin
. . . in fact, although we are all different in
so many ways, football is something that is
common between us. In playing and

celebrating football, all these differences
don't matter, and that's why this sport is such
a good way of bringing people together.'

The Polish families started the applause
this time. Ryan looked at his host mum and
smiled at her. She smiled back.

After they'd eaten, Steve came over to Ryan.

'You OK, Ryan?'

'Yes, Steve,' Ryan said quietly.

He was nervous of Steve. It was the first
time they'd spoken since he'd stripped him
of the captaincy.

'I'd like to ask you to do something for
me.'

'Anything,' Ryan said, desperate to let
Steve know he was sorry.

'As team captain at this tournament it's
your job to hand out the player of the
tournament award.'

'OK,' Ryan said.

'Are you happy to do that?'

'Yes, definitely.' Ryan glowed inside. He knew, of course, who deserved the player of the tournament: Tomasz. And he also knew that this was something he was going to do right. 'But can you give me ten minutes?'

Ten minutes later, after a long conversation with his host mum, Ryan stood next to Steve at the head of the table.

Steve quietened everyone down. 'I'd like to hand over to our team captain, Ryan, who will be presenting the United player of the tournament award.'

Ryan stood up, coughed, then began: '*Z wielką przyjemnością prezentuję graczowi nagrodę tournamentu . . .*' He smiled. 'For those of you who don't speak Polish, I said: It gives me great pleasure to present the player of the tournament award to . . .'

Ryan stopped.

There was a moment's silence, then laughter and applause from both the Polish and English people listening.

Ryan put his hand up. 'To . . . Tomasz.'

And, with that, he held out a small trophy. And the audience applauded wildly.

Finally

Ryan led his team on to the pitch for the final. They ran out alongside the Polish team, Legia Warsaw. It was another clear day. But cold. Just how Ryan liked it.

As they stood in the centre for the team photo, Ryan noticed the Italian and Spanish players standing on the sidelines, all applauding. And an audience of hundreds.

He'd never played in front of such a big crowd.

He felt proud. To be captain of a team in this final. Even if it was the last time he would be captain. He was going to give it his all.

*

Legia had grown in confidence as a team throughout the tournament. After losing so heavily to United, they'd beaten both Madrid and Milan three–two.

Their confidence showed.

Instead of defending, Legia attacked. Even if they did leave themselves open at the back.

Legia scored first. A free kick just outside the area, after Connor had brought down a Polish midfielder.

But, on the stroke of half-time, United equalized. Jake crossed the ball to the far post. Yunis headed it in.

In the second half it was end to end. Ben nearly scored with a low shot from the left. Then Legia had a ten-minute spell that ended with six shots on goal, Tomasz dealing with them all.

But, with ten minutes to go, a Legia player broke through the United defence. And into the penalty area. Connor went to tackle again, right in front of Tomasz, but he missed the ball. And took the boy down.

Another foul.

But this time it wasn't a free kick: it was a penalty.

Tomasz had faced penalties before. He had a good record. Seventeen faced. Only eight goals conceded. Less than half.

But this was the most important one ever. This was a game that mattered.

It meant winning or losing the final.

Tomasz took his place on the goal line and began to breathe slowly. Three deep breaths. He felt calm. And focused. He looked into the eyes of the striker – and sensed a slight fear.

Strikers either took penalties like they knew they were going to score. Or like they were afraid they were going to miss.

This one was afraid.

Tomasz shifted on his feet as the player took two steps up to the ball.

The ball went to Tomasz's right.

Tomasz went to his right.

He reached out and touched the ball with the tip of his fingers. And he thought he'd kept the ball out, but as he hit the ground, he saw the striker turn and raise his arm.

Then Tomasz saw Ryan's shoulders drop. He'd been running into the area to clear the ball if his keeper saved it.

And Tomasz knew.

They were losing two–one. He'd *not* saved the penalty.

Ryan put his hand out to Tomasz. To help him stand.

Tomasz felt himself being pulled up.

'Nice try,' Ryan said. 'You got a hand to it.'

And Tomasz smiled.

United did not score an equalizer.

The game ended two–one.

Tomasz wanted to go off the pitch. He
felt sad. If *only* he'd got to the penalty. But
preparations were being made for the
trophy presentation. A table set out at the
centre of the pitch. A rack of medals. And
the trophy.

And there – again – was Tomasz
Milosz.

Saturday 19 November
Legia Warsaw 2 United 1
Goals: Yunis
Bookings: none

Under-twelves manager's marks out of ten for each player:

Tomasz	7
Connor	6
James	6
Ryan	8
Craig	6
Chi	7
Sam	5
Will	6
Jake	6
Yunis	8
Ben	7

Medals

Steve came round and talked to all the United players.

'Come on, lads. Don't be downhearted. You did United proud. We got to the final. And lost to the home team. There's no shame in that.'

Then Steve went over to Ryan.

'OK?'

'Yeah,' Ryan said. 'Disappointed.'

Steve nodded. 'You did well out there today. I'm proud of you.'

Ryan grinned. 'Thanks, Steve.'

'I mean it. You did well. You've really grown up on this trip.' Steve glanced over to the table where the presentation was to take place. 'It's about to start, Ryan. We'll be first up. Losers' medals. If you sort the lads out, lead them up, then shake hands with Tomasz Milosz, then move on. OK?'

'Sure,' Ryan said.

Two minutes later Ryan gathered the team to receive their runner-ups' medals. For the last time. He would be captain no more. He lined them up. First himself. Then Tomasz. Then the rest.

They stood, waiting on the grass, the sun starting to break through the clouds.

'Tomasz?' Ryan said.

'Yeah?'

'Would you like to lead the team up?'

'What? Really?'

Tomasz looked genuinely thrilled. Ryan could tell.

'Do you want to?' Ryan said.

'I do,' Tomasz said, and shook his captain's hand.

Tomasz Milosz smiled as he saw Tomasz approaching him. He shook Tomasz's hand. Tomasz hung his head and the goalkeeper put the medal round his neck.

'You were unlucky with the penalty,' he said. 'I saw you get a hand to it.'

'Thank you,' Tomasz said.

'Keep it up. One day you may wear the Poland shirt.'

Tomasz smiled. 'I hope so.' Then he turned to Ryan. 'This is our team captain, Ryan.'

Ryan hung his head and felt the losers' medal placed around his neck.

Then Tomasz Milosz shook Ryan's hand. 'You should be very proud of your team. You did well. Maybe I'll see you in an *England* shirt one day?'

Ryan smiled. 'I hope so too. Maybe one day in Poland again. I'd like that.'

Thank Yous

The Football Academy series came about
thanks to the imagination and hard work of
Sarah Hughes, Alison Dougal and Helen
Levene at Puffin, working with David Luxton
at Luxton Harris Literary Agency. Thanks are
due to all four for giving me this opportunity.

Thanks also to Wendy Tse for all
her hard work with the fine detail, and to
everyone at Puffin for all they do: including
Reetu Kabra, Adele Minchin, Louise
Heskett, Sarah Kettle and Tom Sanderson.

Thanks also to Brian Williamson for the great cover image and illustrations.

I needed a lot of help to make sure the academy at 'United' was as close to an English football club's academy as possible. Burnley Football Club let me come to training and matches at their Gawthorpe Hall training ground to watch the under-twelves. Vince Overson and Jeff Taylor gave me lots of time at Burnley and I am extremely grateful. I was also given excellent advice by Kit Carson and Steve Cooper.

Ralph Newbrook at the Football Foundation, also a former youth player for Cambridge United, gave me loads of advice and read the finished manuscript. He – more than anyone – has helped me make this book and series more realistic. Thank you, Ralph!

Huge thanks to my writing group in

Leeds – James Nash and Sophie Hannah. And thanks to Renata Bobik-Dawes and Jonathan Wilson for help with this book.

Finally, thank you to Iris, for being there, and Rebecca, who, as the first reader of my books, always offers intelligent and honest feedback that helps me to shape it.

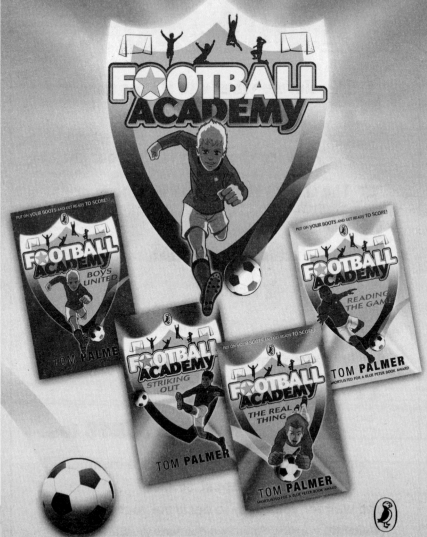

It all started with a Scarecrow

Puffin is well over sixty years old.
Sounds ancient, doesn't it? But Puffin has never been
so lively. We're always on the lookout for the next big
idea, which is how it began all those years ago.

Penguin Books was a big idea from the mind of
a man called Allen Lane, who in 1935 invented
the quality paperback and changed the world.
**And from great Penguins, great Puffins grew,
changing the face of children's books forever.**

The first four Puffin Picture Books were hatched in 1940 and the
first Puffin story book featured a man with broomstick arms called
Worzel Gummidge. In 1967 Kaye Webb, Puffin Editor, started the
Puffin Club, promising to **'make children into readers'.**
She kept that promise and over 200,000 children became
devoted Puffineers through their quarterly installments of
Puffin Post, which is now back for a new generation.

Many years from now, we hope you'll look back and
remember Puffin with a smile. **No matter what your age
or what you're into, there's a Puffin for everyone.**
The possibilities are endless, but one thing is for sure:
whether it's a picture book or a paperback, a sticker book
or a hardback, **if it's got that little Puffin
on it – it's bound to be good.**

Puffin by Post

Football Academy: The Real Thing – Tom Palmer

If you have enjoyed this book and want to read more,
then check out these other great Puffin titles.
You can order any of the following books direct with Puffin by Post:

Football Academy: Boys United • Tom Palmer • 9780141324678   £4.99

The first in an exciting, fast-paced series.

Football Academy: Striking Out • Tom Palmer • 9780141324685   £4.99

More Academy action in this second story in the series.

Football Academy: Reading the Game • Tom Palmer • 9780141324708 £4.99

Stay on the ball with the fourth book in the series.

Jake Cake: The Football Beast • Michael Broad • 9780141323701   £4.99

Jake Cake's wild and unbelievable adventures.

Football Detective: Foul Play • Tom Palmer • 9780141323671   £5.99

For 9+. Shortlisted for the 2009 Blue Peter Awards.

Just contact:

Puffin Books, C/o Bookpost, PO Box 29,
Douglas, Isle of Man, IM99 1BQ
Credit cards accepted. For further details:
Telephone: 01624 677237
Fax: 01624 670923

You can email your orders to: bookshop@enterprise.net
Or order online at: www.bookpost.co.uk

Free delivery in the UK.
Overseas customers must add £2 per book.

Prices and availability are subject to change.

Visit puffin.co.uk to find out about the latest titles, read extracts and
exclusive author interviews, and enter exciting competitions.
You can also browse thousands of Puffin books online.